11.95

Santa Claus Forever!

by Carolyn Haywood

illustrated by Glenys and Victor Ambrus

William Morrow and Company
New York • 1983

The artists and the author
unite in dedicating
this book with affection
to
Connie Epstein

Text copyright © 1983 by Carolyn Haywood
Illustrations copyright © 1983 by Glenys and Victor Ambrus
All rights reserved. No part of this book may be reproduced or utilized in any form or by any means, electronic or
mechanical, including photocopying, recording or by any information storage and retrieval system, without permission
in writing from the Publisher. Inquiries should be addressed to William Morrow and Company, Inc., 105 Madison Avenue,
New York, N.Y. 10016.
Printed in the United States of America.

1   2   3   4   5   6   7   8   9   10

Library of Congress Cataloging in Publication Data
Haywood, Carolyn, 1898–   Santa Claus forever!
Summary: After a particularly difficult Christmas Eve, Santa decides to retire, but when he sees his replacement, he changes
his mind. [1. Santa Claus—Fiction. 2. Christmas—Fiction]   I. Ambrus, Glenys, ill. II. Ambrus, Victor G., ill. III. Title.
PZ7.H31496San   1983   [E]   83-1017
ISBN 0-688-02344-4
ISBN 0-688-02345-2 (lib. bdg.)

On the day before Christmas, Santa Claus picked up
his last sack of mail at the North Pole Post Office.

He had received more letters this year than ever before.
They had come from all over the world.

Dear Santa Claus,
Please bring me a pony.
How could he get a pony down a chimney?

Dear Santa Claus,
Please, may I go with you to the moon
on Christmas Eve? I want to be an astronaut.
But the moon was not on his route yet.

Dear Santa Claus,
Please bring me a baby brother.
Baby brothers could not be put into stockings.

Santa felt sad, as he always did when he
couldn't make someone happy.

There was a letter from a little girl asking for a red-haired doll. Santa Claus wondered whether he had any left.

There was one from a boy asking for a blue dump truck, not pale blue—dark blue. Santa Claus scratched his head. He had orange dump trucks and red dump trucks, but he knew he didn't have any blue dump trucks.

These last-minute requests seemed harder and harder to fill.

Santa went to his toy shop and looked over the dolls. There were blond ones, brown-haired ones, and black-haired ones, but no redheads. One of the blond dolls would have to be turned into a redhead.

Santa mixed some red dye in a little bowl and with a piece of cotton dyed the hair of one of the blond dolls. Some dye splashed on his white beard. He picked up a rag and tried to wipe it off, but instead he smeared it.

"Oh, no!" he said. "What a mess."

Next he had to do something about the little boy's dump truck. Santa Claus picked up a can of blue paint and one of the orange dump trucks. But as he removed the lid from the paint, he knocked over the can. He had to stop and wipe up the spill with a rag.

"I'm glad these things dry quickly, or I'd be in a fix this Christmas Eve," he said to himself. "Now I have to try to get cleaned up." He got a bottle of turpentine and went to work. He removed most of the paint and dye from his fingers. There was no time to do anything about his beard.

It was time to pack up the toys and hitch up his reindeer. But in the stable, he found one lying on the ground. Santa knelt beside the reindeer. Its nose felt hot and dry. "You don't feel well, do you?" said Santa." "You are not going tonight. We'll just have to manage with seven reindeer."

At last he climbed into his sleigh, cracked his whip, and off they flew.

At the first roof, the sleigh banged against the chimney.
One of the runners was bent.

"Too bad, but I can't fix this until I get home," Santa said.
"We'll have a lot of bumpy takeoffs and landings tonight."

When Santa stepped into the chimney flue of the next house, he saw that there were still embers lying in the fireplace. "Oh, no!" cried Santa Claus. But it was too late. There was no way to avoid the hot coals. The next thing Santa knew his pants were on fire.

Santa hurried out the front door and sat down in a snowdrift. The wet snow snuffed out his burning trousers, leaving him with a scorched smell.

Santa Claus took off for another chimney. There were no embers in it, but a loose brick fell down and hit him on the head. "What a night!" Santa said, rubbing his head. "I'll be lucky if I get home alive!"

At last, after many stops, Santa Claus returned to the North Pole. He sat down in his easy chair and drank a cup of hot chocolate as he soaked his cold feet in a tub of warm water. "This was quite a Christmas Eve! A sick reindeer, a dented runner, burned pants, and a brick on my head." Santa groaned. "I am so tired," he said. "I'm all done in."

He began to think back over past Christmases. When he tried to count, he lost track of the number. "How time flies!" he said. "I'm getting to be a very old man. Perhaps it's time for me to retire."

Why shouldn't I? he thought. No more mountains of letters, no more last-minute toys to be made, no more burned trousers. The more he thought about it, the better he liked the idea. He would let the world know right away.

Santa Claus reached for the telephone and dialed one of the television networks. "This is Santa Claus," he said to the man who answered. "I have an announcement to make. I'm retiring, and I want you to spread the news around the world....What?...You say, 'We can't have a world without Santa Claus?'...Now don't try to change my mind. I'm going to retire, and I mean it!"

Santa Claus almost did change his mind when he received an avalanche of letters from children begging him not to retire. Santa was touched. Still, he remembered, it was so much hard work. He wasn't as young as he used to be.

A week later, on New Year's Eve, a snowstorm was raging outside. Santa Claus was snoozing restfully by the fire, when he heard the sound of a low-flying plane. Not long afterward, the sleigh bells at the front door rang.

As Santa opened the front door, an icy blast blew into the room. There stood a strange figure, dressed exactly like Santa.

Santa couldn't believe his eyes. "Who are you?" he exclaimed.

"Good evening," said the stranger. "I'm the new Santa Claus. May I come in?"

"Why y-y-yes," Santa stammered. "Come in and sit down."

The visitor came in and made himself comfortable in a chair across from Santa Claus. "This is certainly a hard place to get to," the stranger complained. "Plenty of planes flying over the North Pole, but none lands here except the mail plane. I had to bail out in a parachute."

"Why did you come here?" Santa Claus asked.

"I flew up here to look the place over," replied the stranger. "You can show me around and help me get started. I have some changes in mind, of course, and I'm eager to begin."

"Changes?" said Santa Claus. "What kind of changes?"

"Well, in the first place, I'm not going to bother with children's letters. From now on, the letters go into the scrap basket. Nor do I intend to spend all my time taking children on my lap and talking to them when I visit department stores. I have to move around the toy department and see how sales are going." Then he winked at Santa and said, "And there are some children I don't care for. So I'll just put coal in their stockings, if I visit them at all. I'm going to concentrate on children who get good grades in school."

Santa Claus leaped from his chair. "No, no!" he cried. "A thousand no's! You can't treat my children that way! Who made you Santa Claus, I'd like to know?"

"I'm from the Mega-Fun Corporation, the world's largest toy company. This is a very important promotion for me!"

"Pooh, Pooh," said Santa Claus. "I know that company. Very inferior product. The children will never be pleased with those toys. They want toys made by Santa Claus. Oh, what have I done?"

"You've retired," said the new Santa Claus.

"I have *not* retired!" said Santa Claus, stamping his foot. "I can see my plan was a terrible mistake." He began to pace back and forth. "I'm the real Santa Claus. How could I leave my children to an impostor who doesn't love them all, who plays favorites, and puts coal in their stockings!"

The visitor jumped up. "But you said you wanted to retire. Times are changing and —"

"Never mind," said Santa Claus. "There's only one Santa Claus! I'm the real Santa, and I'll be Santa Claus forever!"

"Well, that leaves me out in the cold, doesn't it?" said the visitor. "Maybe I'm not so keen on the job anyhow. It seems like a lot of hard work."

Santa nodded his head. "It takes love and love and more love," he said. He offered his hand to the visitor, saying, "Well, Happy New Year to you."

As they shook hands, the visitor smiled. "Happy New Year to you, Santa Claus."

The news flashed around the world that Santa Claus had not retired. It was a glorious New Year's Eve. Children who had gone to bed early were wakened by their parents and told the good news. They threw off their covers and bounced up and down on their beds shouting, "Hurrah! Hurrah! Santa Claus will come again and again forever!" Bells rang and whistles blew all over the world.

About the Author

Carolyn Haywood was born in Philadelphia and now lives in Chestnut Hill, a suburb of that city. A graduate of the Philadelphia Normal School, she also studied at the Pennsylvania Academy of Fine Arts, where she won the Cresson European Scholarship. Her first story, *"B" Is for Betsy*, was published in 1939. Since then she has written books almost every year and has become one of the most widely read American writers for younger children.

About the Artists

Victor Ambrus was born in Budapest, Hungary, and Glenys Ambrus in London, England. Both are graduates of the Royal College of Art, in London, and are noted illustrators. Mr. Ambrus won the 1965 Kate Greenaway Medal in England for his picture book *Three Poor Tailors* and won again in 1975 for his two books *Horses in Battle* and *Mishka*. Victor and Glenys Ambrus live in Surrey, England.